TEN
LITTLE
ELVES

For Emily - our own little Christmas Elf
M.B.

For Erin & Isla
S.R.

ORCHARD BOOKS

First published in Great Britain in 2016 by The Watts Publishing Group
This edition first published in 2020

1 3 5 7 9 10 8 6 4 2

Text © Mike Brownlow, 2016
Illustrations © Simon Rickerty, 2016

A CIP catalogue record for this book is available from the British Library.
ISBN 978 1 40836 249 5
Printed and bound in China

Orchard Books
An imprint of Hachette Children's Group
Part of The Watts Publishing Group Limited
Carmelite House
50 Victoria Embankment
London EC4Y 0DZ

An Hachette UK Company
www.hachette.co.uk

www.hachettechildrens.co.uk

TEN LITTLE ELVES

MIKE BROWNLOW SIMON RICKERTY

ORCHARD

Ten little Christmas elves

are making toys until . . .

. . . Santa shouts, "The reindeer!

HELP!

I think they're really ill!

We need the magic cough drops from the Reindeer Doctor's cave.

Can you fetch them, little elves?
Then Christmas will be saved!"

Ten little Christmas elves
think they've found a sign.

10

Now there are . . .

"WOOF!"

goes the husky team.

. . . nine.

Nine little Christmas elves,
getting in a state.

"WHAAAAH!"

Snowballs everywhere!

Now there are . . .

...eight.

**Eight little Christmas elves,
gazing up to heaven.**

8

. . . **seven.**

Seven little Christmas
elves in a silly fix.

7

"YOO-EE-OOO!"

a yeti yowls.

Now there are . . .

. . . six.

Six little Christmas elves
make a desperate dive.

6

BRRRRR!

blows the icy storm.

Now there are . . .

. . . **five.**

Five little Christmas elves
stand in shock and awe!

5

...four.

4

Four little Christmas elves rest
near Jack Frost's tree.

CLINK!

go the icicles.

Now there are . . .

...three.

Three little Christmas elves
find the Doctor's! Phew!

3

WHOOMF!

goes a fall of snow.

Now there are . . .

...two.

Two little Christmas elves,
on the homeward run.

2

CRACK!

goes the splitting ice.

Now there's only . . .

...one.

One little Christmas elf,
trudging through the snow,

1

Nearly out of energy,
what's that distant glow?

It's Santa's Grotto!
HIP HOORAY!
Her efforts weren't in vain.

**The reindeer munch the cough drops
- now they all feel fine again!**

They load the sleigh,

then **1, 2, 3**

and **UP** into the air,

Soon they'll be delivering

their presents everywhere!

High above the silvery clouds
the elf and Santa climb.

But they'll be back before too long and then it's

party time!

"Congratulations little elves!
You've just saved Christmas Day!"

Ten little Christmas elves all say,

"**YAY!**"

MERRY CHRISTMAS